CW00642722

We're Worried About Him

Liam Gilliver

Copyright © 2012 Liam Gilliver

All rights reserved.

ISBN: 9781728615059

DEDICATION

This book is dedicated to all the boys who have been in my life, who, whether small or significant, have shaped my idea of love and heartbreak, and have changed me into who I am today. You may not know the effect you have all had on me. But I hope you read this and learn how much, at one point, you all meant to me.

Liam Gilliver

CONTENTS

ACKNOWLEDGMENTS

I would like to give my sincere thanks to Emma Wigston for proofreading this entire book; for staying in Starbucks with me week in and week out until it closed to ensure we put every comma and semi colon in the right place, for laughing at my unfortunate typos, and making this book as eloquent and flawless as it could ever be. I mean, you even proofread this. I will be forever grateful for your commitment.

I also owe a massive thank you to Emma Laird. Without you, I'm not sure this book would have been completed. In fact, without you it would be nothing more than a dream. You have been unfailingly supportive of my decision to self-publish, have motivated me on days when I have wanted to give up, and have spent hours reading my work and giving me inspiration.

This cover was designed by the talented Rosy Nash - thank you for creating something as beautiful as the story itself.

And a final thank you to everyone who has bought this book and shown interest in my work. I'm excited for you to connect with the characters how I intended, and hope this book serves as just one more representation for queer people.

Liam Gilliver

1. CLEMENTINE

he changes with the seasons

pale in the winter

freckled in the spring

tanned in the summer

and by the time autumn comes

his hair is long enough to tie off his face

but no matter how much the universe changes him

or allows him to grow

his eyes remain the same

just how trees always keep their roots

even if they lose everything else

- grounded

I met him in Venice, somewhere between Saint Mark's Basillica and what soon became our favourite ristorante, Bistrot De Venise. He guided me through the city, with the water to our right, and an endless row of boutiques selling Murano glass to our left.

"Here, try this on." He took my hand and slid a marbled ring from a small shop called L'isola on my middle finger. I looked up at him, and he squeezed my hand tightly. I wasn't sure what to say - it was only a ring after all - but the warmth from his touch seem to spread through my body, lingering still even when the moment had passed.

As it hit midday, we couldn't escape the sun: its rays penetrated down in the plaza, turning the canals into a shade of emerald I never knew existed. I couldn't tell whether the streets were becoming narrower, or if it was just the crowds of tourists flocking from the harbour that quickly made it difficult to stroll companionably.

We ended that night in an old-fashioned pizzeria, located in one of the quiet streets just outside the centre. We drank wine we couldn't pronounce whilst sat on the veranda, positioned above the people who were only just discovering the same streets we had ventured down a few hours ago. Conversation with him was always so nonchalant, and yet still held me so that the disappointment was crushing when I realised the speed with which the time so often passed; every time I glanced at my watch I sighed. The waiters knew not to disturb us, and even when the place was about to close no one interrupted with the bill.

Per amore, aspetteremo - for love, we'll wait

I soon realised Venice was a city that had time for you, one that didn't rush or wait impatiently for you to leave. In many ways it was a reminder of a simpler time, one that made me nostalgic for memories I was too young to actually recall. People still used answering machines and flip phones, music was played on cassettes, Kodak camera shops sold film, and cafés were decorated with red canopies which prevented the sun's rays from reaching the pavement.

That summer we lived and breathed the Italian lifestyle, sleeping in the colours of red, white, and green - colours that perhaps should have felt alien to us, but didn't. I never thought about home, only its inevitably daunting arrival that crept closer with each sun kissed day. This was now my routine, my life: him; the orange trees outside our apartment that never became bare, though I picked and squeezed them for breakfast every morning; the art, concealed in buildings that in themselves were masterpieces, from Galleria Bevilazqua La Masa to Giudecca 795, and the aroma of the coffee served black in hand-painted mugs. Even the days spent hiding from the heat, lay on crisp linen with the patio doors open, letting the air-con settle onto my skin, too hot to even move, were better than anything home could offer.

Home. That word soon lost its meaning; in fact, that summer most things lost their meaning. It was only here that I could truly escape the almost traumatic effects of my tiring obsession to chase perfection and success, and my willingness to do things I really didn't want to because I really thought I should. They all became nothing more than figments of the past, and a reminder that nothing really mattered in the end.

I was a writer, never making much money from it, in spite of the sporadic commissions from magazines. So I picked up a few shifts at the local bar, serving old men with cigars and unbuttoned shirts; espressos in the day and pints of beer when the afternoon came. The owner didn't pay much, but the tips were good, and one of the waiters improved my Italian in exchange for help with his English. I benefited more; his English was already perfect.

I would write about him when I wasn't working, and he would sing about me. He was aiming for success as a singer, and, whilst he wasn't popular to the world, his voice became the only thing I could listen to - never tiring, never unwanted. Those melodies would play in my head as we went out to eat, or stayed in to try and recreate the dishes we fell in love with from the menus of our favourite restaurants. They remained when we fell asleep together, and when we strolled through new parts of the city we visited on recommendation. And when we fucked, the melody only got louder. My moans turned into the vibrations of a cello, like he was plucking at the strings of my body. I gasped his name to the rhythm of his movements, and my favourite chorus, the one I never got bored of, was his cum inside me.

It was the end of July, and the sun didn't want to set until after nine. The amber glow from the sky was replaced by the tip of my cigarette, carelessly resting between my lips as he held his lighter close to me, carefully sheltering the flame with his hand. Silence was rare here, but there were brief moments when the music and church bells both stopped, moments when I inhaled, focussing only on the faint crackling of my cigarette.

"Silence," I always observed. The air was still warm, but the contrast from the day made me feel cold, or as cold as you could possibly be in 20 degrees. He placed his leather jacket over my shoulders, and in exchange I passed him my half-smoked cigarette.

"You know, we should talk," he exhaled, and I watched the white cloud of smoke evaporate into the air, following its trail as if waiting for it to lead me to a reply.

"Doesn't mean we have to," I answered, which meant I was scared. Scared to talk about whatever it was we weren't talking about. Our relationship, his sexuality, home, not being right here right now: they were all things we didn't want to discuss - unknown and unwelcome. Even coming to the end of a cigarette evoked fear; fear that now

I had no excuse to stay next to him, sat on the floor, thinking about nothing.

"I finished that book," he said, a welcome diversion. I smiled as well as I could, but the sudden solemnity I felt from that exchange was too overwhelming to simply shake off. I had given him my copy of Wilde's Dorian Gray a few weeks prior to that night, as it was the novel that carried me through my teenage years and originally sparked my interest in writing. It was now tattered, with highlighted quotes and coffee stains on most of the pages.

"What did you think?" I turned my head towards him to see him stubbing out his cigarette and smirking. Of course he loved it. Why wouldn't he?

"Best one yet," he replied. I guess it was easier to talk about fiction, about characters that only existed in our minds, ones that we could think about whilst reading, before discarding them beside our beds at night to forget about. If only we could navigate our own lives through chapters and page numbers. Maybe things would have been easier to cope with if I had been able to cherry-pick which parts of our relationship I was able to revel in, simply discounting the others as bad chapters. And if I had skipped to the last page and found a twist I didn't like, I guess I would have stopped reading.

he spits on my chest

then rubs it dry with the heel of his palm

while my sweat sinks

into his sheets

like we are exchanging parts of us

without even realising

- unbeknown

The next morning my mind was empty; only Venice could have that effect on me. My thumb was black from abusing my lighter the night before, and his fingers were bruised from holding down the chords on his guitar. Usually he played to make his fingers bleed, but last night he was too distracted, too occupied exchanging spit and sweat. I left him in bed and headed to the kitchen with my book, ripping the month of July off the calendar that hung from the wall and folding the page to use as a bookmark. I welcomed August with bitterness and relief: we only had a month left, *but at least we had a month left.* I was reading Cohen's poetry, after being introduced to his work by a friend. As I turned the next page, guitar strings began echoing through the apartment, and soon after I heard his voice singing along to the melody.

"I have good news," he shouted from the bedroom. As much as I knew it couldn't be, part of me wished the news was that we could stay here forever. He came into the kitchen, grinning so hard he had laughter lines cutting deep at either side of his face. That grin was contagious, and though I knew his news wasn't what I wanted, I smiled back in anticipation.

"We're going on tour."

My heart plummeted, further than it ever had before. We were leaving Venice, sooner than I had thought. And he was happy about it. This was everything he wanted - there was no way I couldn't support him. There was, however, a small part of me that wondered if Venice would still be the same if he wasn't there. Would those morning oranges still be sweet if squeezed into only one glass, when even the thought of it left a bitter taste in my mouth? My love for both him and Venice were hazily entwined, so much so that it didn't seem possible to separate them. It's where we first met, first kissed, first fucked. If I left with him, Venice would still be there. But if I left him, he could be gone forever, and that was something I would never dare test.

In my mind I had made a future for us here. There

was a pastel pink casa situated on the River degli Schiavoni, standing proudly amongst the gothic architecture and Venice's famous gondolas. Every time I walked past I thought about who lived there, how good it must feel to open the white shutters every morning and look across the water, standing on the gated black balcony that offered those spectacular views at such spectacular height. Sometimes I even considered climbing up to the balcony, throwing my legs over, seeing how good it would feel to let go of the railings and fall. Then I felt guilty, so I thought about him, about *us*, and the possibility of living there one day. We rarely spoke about the future - I guess it was another thing that should have been on the agenda but remained something we ignored out of fear.

He did mention once the possibility of us opening a small edicola in one of the smaller sub-sections of the city, selling Italian magazines to locals and postcards to tourists.

"You could carry on writing, and I could carry on singing, and the nights would be ours," he'd pledged. But those plans were built on the idea that we'd be here forever, and now that idea was crumbling in front of me.

"We're starting in LA," he said, breaking the silence, and my daydream came to an abrupt halt.

"Great," I lied. Not great, not great at all. I didn't want palm trees and beaches - I wanted Venice. I wanted him in Venice. Us in Venice.

"Are you sure?" he asked, most likely sensing disappointment in my half-hearted smile.

"You know I'd choose you. Every time," I said. It was true. I was his. Like a branding iron to skin, I was seared to him. The next thing I knew we were packing our scarce belongings into our suitcases. They'd been left open on the apartment floor since we got here, a bad omen which served to remind me that our time there could never last.

I had started rolling our cigarettes instead of buying them, because there was something about it that just seemed more personal.

"Seeing you with something I made in your mouth is heavenly."

He grinned in response, and for a second I forgot that was the day we were leaving Venice.

* * *

We headed to Treviso, a city north of where we'd been living. We only stayed there one night as our flight was in the early hours of the morning. I was grateful for Treviso, viewing it as a gradual release from the true summer we were leaving behind. The buildings were similar, canals still wound through the streets, and the wine we tasted was still just as crisp. But there were noticeable differences; the heat was less intense, the air was lighter, and there were significantly fewer people in comparison to the hustle that could be found alongside the Grand Canal.

"At least we escaped the tourists," he quipped. It was exactly what I was thinking, and I replied with a small laugh.

"Places like this are always unappreciated," I shrugged in response. It was true; even we were leaving before the sun had a chance to rise. Most of the tourists only flew there because of the low costs, and the only big groups of people that could be seen were outside the train station, as if there was nothing there of any worth: an observation that was both unfair and untrue.

"We should come back here one day," I suggested, immediately regretting my words. I don't think I could have handled going so close to Venice again, without actually returning there to relive its splendour. But he agreed, nodding his head, and my regret eased.

2. BLOOD ORANGE

We flew to Los Angeles, replacing canals with highways, pizzerias for service station food, and our treasured apartment with its orange trees outside for cheap motels haunted by prostitutes. But my love for him only grew stronger, maybe because there were less distractions, and nothing to do before he went on stage - so we reminisced a lot, fucked a lot, smoked a lot, and slowly adjusted to our new life on the road.

Ci siamo acclimatati - we acclimatised

We stopped over at a motel just outside of Silverlake in Los Angeles, a simple two-storey building situated on the corner, opposite a worn out service station and pizza shop that appeared to open and close at consistently irregular times.

"So this is home for the next few nights?" I observed bleakly, with a hesitance in my voice that questioned whether I could really deal with it. The arm that he placed around my shoulder went a little way in relieving some of the doubt that was evident in my tone.

"For now," he said, squeezing me tighter, "but home is wherever we choose to go." He was right, and I felt ashamed for my pessimistic outlook. He checked us in while I sat outside and smoked, watching as a family pulled up and got out of the car. The father insisted the place 'would do' but the children seemed unimpressed, pointing out with distaste that the neon sign was flickering like the beginning of a horror film.

I'm not sure how long I sat there, but the sky had turned much darker, and there hadn't been a car pull in for fuel in a while. There were no stars in sight, just a black blanket that smothered any remaining light.

"Shit!" I panicked as the ash from my cigarette fell onto the bare flesh exposed by the rip in my jeans. I stood up quickly to brush it off, but it had already etched itself into my skin, leaving a searing pain that seemed to wrap itself around my thigh. I started to cry, and thought about how this would never have happened in Venice. I wasn't sure whether I'd done it on purpose, whether part of me knew the ash would fall and hurt me, and I didn't care - that was enough to scare me. I walked up to the second floor, entering our room with its bland terracotta walls and yellow bedding. My eyes searched for any reminder of Venice, but there was nothing, so I started to cry harder.

"What's up?" He put down his bourbon and wrapped his arms around me, and for the first time his touch didn't stop the flow of my tears. The ash had made an ugly yellow burn mark on my thigh, and I whimpered when the cold denim of his jeans touched it, commanding his attention.

"What did you do?" He looked down with concern and anger in his eyes, clearly thinking it was self-inflicted. He traced his fingers around the burn, gentle enough to cause no pain. I still couldn't speak through the tears, so he laid me down on the bed and held me tight. When my head hit the flat pillow, I realised how tired I was. Really fucking tired. I hadn't slept in over 40 hours: maybe that was why I'd not reacted downstairs and caught the falling ash.

Maybe it *was* a mistake.
        "Shut your eyes," he said "It's going be alright."
I didn't know what he was referring to in particular, but I did as he said and shut my eyes regardless. I thought about us living in Venice with its maze of canals, the city that thrived on nothing but water. I turned my face towards his, my eyes still closed. "Rock me?"

I didn't wake until gone ten, and I'm sure it probably would have been later, but the cleaners eventually knocked and disturbed my deep sleep. The burn on my thigh had already scabbed over, but remained too tender to touch. There was a note from him on the bedside cabinet:

'Checking out the venue for tonight, hope you slept well. I love you x'

I sat on the balcony, drinking water from the only bottle I still had left with an Italian label.
        God, how pathetic.
        I looked at my new uninspiring view of an apartment block above the pizza shop. I saw an old woman with red hair and heavy earrings, who hung outside her window to clean her rug, banging it against the wall with such severity that I flinched each time she did so. Below her were two heavily tattooed men who sat playing cards; both overweight, both grey-haired. I wondered what their relationship was; whether they were brothers, lovers, bikers, divorced men who hated their ex-wives for taking their houses, men who loved whiskey more than they did women, or maybe even men that had never loved. My eyes were still sore from last night's tears. Maybe if I had been able to distinguish their tattoos, it would have revealed more about their relationship. Not that it even mattered. I contemplated whether they had looked up and tried to

decipher my story: 'check it out, it's that 20-year-old boy who burnt himself in the car park and cried all night.'

When he returned from the venue I was in the bathroom, sitting naked on the floor against the tub. I was waiting for it to fill, just enough so the water would cover my chest but keep my forearms dry to enable me to read. He followed the sound of the water.

"Oh, I could get used to this," he said, smirking at my naked body. I laughed, and rolled my eyes affectionately at his audacity.

"How were rehearsals?" I asked, flinching as I checked the temperature.

"Too hot?" he asked, laughing. "It's a small venue, but it's a good start I suppose. I just hope enough people will turn up to fill it." His voice lacked confidence, and it was disconcerting to see him so unusually vulnerable.

"It's your first night, don't worry," I assured him. He didn't reply, just watched as I stepped into the tub, hanging my legs out of the water so the heat wasn't overwhelming. He sighed and sat on the floor against the side of the bath, taking one of his hands and slowly rubbing it up and down my leg: half dry, half wet.

"I wrote a song about you: maybe you could finish the gig with it?" I suggested.
The rubbing stopped, and he looked at me with a defensive glare, as if already annoyed at what I was about to say. "What's it about?"

"That girl."

"I thought you were over that?"

"I am."

"So you wrote a song about it?"

"I am now," I said. "I'm over it *now*."

His jaw was tight, and there was a tension in the air that made it difficult to breathe. The water didn't help, irritating the burn on my leg and making it itch unbearably, tides of pain that broke the silence.

* * *

The song was about this girl in Venice who worked at the same bar as me for a while. I can't remember her name, just her long dark hair and red velvet lips. She was American, and was only in Italy over the summer as part of her scholarship to study abroad. She never said why she worked; instead she constantly reminded us about her father's wealth and how he was subsidising her central apartment near St Marks. Probably something about 'character building'.

* * *

It was the night after we'd first slept together: the night I lost my virginity to him. As awkward and painful as it was, it felt right, satisfying an urge I never realised I had. But I couldn't help feeling like I had sacrificed everything for someone who'd done this time and time before.

We'd been drinking since nine, celebrating the bar's fifth anniversary with an all-night lock in. I'd only been drunk a few times; I guess the idea of not being in control of my own body had deterred me in the past, but after a few shots were forced into my hand, I said farewell to my sobriety for the night.

"What are you drinking?" He jumped over the bar, knocking over the half-emptied drinks that had been left there. We both laughed, and I hopped onto one of the red leather stools.

"Surprise me." *My first mistake.*

I looked into his tsunami eyes, and those thick unbrushed eyebrows that shadowed them: *my second mistake.* I watched him make an espresso martini, mesmerised by his every move. He was just so... *compelling:* the white scar that rested near his temples, his olive complexion, the perfect waves of his raven hair. Everything about him intrigued me; I should've known right there that I was sat in front of the guy I was about to fall helplessly in love with. He pushed the glass towards me by its thin stem, but kept his hand firmly on it as his brow furrowed. "Wait," he said, before carefully dropping a single coffee bean into the centre of my drink. "Perfect."

"Fucking hell." I screwed my face up after taking the first sip. "How strong is this?" My vision blurred, and all I could do was concentrate on not being sick.

"It's got a kick to it, hasn't it? Don't worry, you'll get used to it." He was right. I took another sip, and another, and another, until eventually the burning sensation in my throat dulled to a numb ache and my glass was nearly empty. My head felt kind of dizzy, and my heart was beating unnervingly fast, but all I could think about was how much I wanted to kiss him. He jumped back over the bar, without spilling a drop of his drink.

"Want to dance?" he asked. I reached out for his hand in response - *my third mistake* - but when I went to stand I lost my balance, and in that split second decision of whether to fall into his arms or onto the floor, I chose him.

We danced into the early hours of the morning. I'd never heard any of the songs that were playing, most of them were in Italian, and I was too drunk to try and translate. His body never broke contact with mine, almost like we were both scared of letting go. People were getting tired and beginning to head home, making the room seem much bigger. But I didn't want the night to end, and kept dancing like it had just begun. The moments of silence between songs were our only opportunities to exchange words. And just after the tacky announcement introducing the night's penultimate song, he asked me: "Come back to mine?"

That was the first time I had been to the apartment, and I couldn't resist grabbing an orange from the tree while he searched his pockets for his keys. The moon was out in all its glory, and the white light seemed to illuminate the key hole, as if urging us to go inside. We stumbled up the stairs, into his bedroom, onto his bed, under the sheets. I think he knew that it was my first time. The alcohol wore off, replaced by nerves that stiffened my body. His touch made me shiver, but not with nerves as he probably thought. I shivered because I knew right then I was falling for somebody who might not even remember my name in the morning.

"Are you sure you want do this?"

"Yes."

honestly,

i never really feel like he is mine

even now

as he holds me in his arms

still not mine

i won't sleep tonight

because i know

when i open my eyes

he'll either be gone

or still be there

and i can't figure out which scares me the most

- possession

The next morning I left without saying goodbye. His eyes were still shut, and light had fought its way through the blinds, casting stripes of shadow across his body. He looked so angelic lying there, his hair perfectly messy, his feet hanging carelessly off the bed. I felt so lucky to have had him, even if just for one night.

I headed to work, with a headache that tormented me my entire shift. My whole body felt bruised, and I flinched hard when a customer needing a refill tapped me on the shoulder. I couldn't help but feel like I'd lost something else last night, a part of my innocence I could never get back, and when I caught a glimpse of my reflection in the mirror it took a while to recognise what was staring back.

"I need to go home." I don't think my boss heard, but I threw my apron over one of the stools at the bar regardless, and left almost three hours before my shift was due to end. The sunlight didn't help my headache and the lump that grew in my throat made it difficult to swallow. So I found refuge halfway between work and my apartment. At the end of the shaded alley stood a man selling bottled water out of a cooler box, surrounded by a crowd of dehydrated tourists that couldn't hack the heat either. And that's where I saw him, kissing that girl, her red velvet lips pressed against his, and his hands buried in her long dark hair - both disguised as tourists. I don't know if he saw me, but I pushed back through the crowd, trying to hold it together until I got to my apartment, then lost all sense of control and threw up violently in the gutter outside.

How fucking stupid could I be?

why her?

why not me?

i can give you so much more

i can give you everything

let me

press my fingers into the dimples on your shoulders

blow air down the arch of your back

feel the shaven hair on the nape of your neck

let me

mercilessly give myself to you

swallow every tear and eat every word

til my bones become so familiar your fingers trace them
perfectly

and if that's still not enough

you can return to her

- part 1: implore

but then i look at you

looking at her

the way i look at you

and suddenly

your body becomes foreign ground

my loving touch an invasion

both

uninvited

unrequited.

- part 2: surrender

I didn't see him for a few weeks after it had happened, most likely because I tried my hardest to reduce the chance of bumping into him. I asked for morning shifts, knowing that he'd still be in bed while I was serving coffee, then after work I headed straight back to the apartment I was renting. It was small and kind of dingy, with uninspiring canvases in every room. And there were no orange trees outside.

A few weeks later, I walked into work and there he was, as comely as I remembered, his hair tied up and still dressed in black. That same leather jacket I took off him in his bedroom was draped over his shoulders, and the same look was in his eyes.

"Have you been avoiding me?"

"Why would I be doing that?" It was a half-hearted deflection; I didn't convince myself, let alone him.

"I don't know, you tell me. You were the one that left."

"Did you expect pancakes in bed?" I surprised myself with how harsh my comment was. Shock flashed across his face; his eyes narrowed and his jaw clenched.

"Shut up and have a drink. You're more pleasant when you're drunk."

I retaliated a thousand times in my head but in reality I said nothing. I simply rolled my eyes at his hurtful remark and let him pour me a drink.

That's how they started again, the drunk one-night stands that neither of us mentioned during the day. It was as if we both had to be intoxicated to admit we were falling for each other, as if the moon granted permission where the sun didn't. But there was always reason to celebrate in Venice - somebody, somewhere had something to party about. Birthdays, anniversaries, Saturday nights; they were all valid excuses to drink to excess and wake up beside one another. Each time, I learned more and more about him: where he studied, his non-existent relationship with his parents, his dreams of becoming a singer. And each time I fell more and more in love with him, so much so that after a while we didn't need alcohol to wet our mouths: the saliva on the corner of his lips was intoxicating enough.

I never asked him about his ex girlfriends, though I'd heard from the rumour mill that they existed in abundance. We just never really spoke about it, and honestly I'm not sure whether I could have anyway.

* * *

And now here he was - reading the song about that girl from the alley while sat against the bath, and all of a sudden the water felt ice cold.

"I like it, it's really good. Really, *really* good."

"You're not mad?"

"No, not if it helped you get over it."

My relief seemed to warm the water, and his hand

found its way back to my leg. Why hadn't I just told him this sooner?

"Can I join you?" He pulled his top over his head, unbuckled his belt and dropped his trousers. It was a routine I witnessed most nights, but, unlike when he was singing on stage, I was his only audience. If it had been appropriate to applaud his beauty I probably would have done so, but as he kicked his underwear to the floor, I sensed his performance wasn't over. The water level rose as he got in, and I wrapped my legs around his waist and felt him slowly ease his way inside me. He was usually always so gentle, always so measured, and the water rocked between us like a calm tide. But there was something different this time, something more menacing, maybe because he'd just finished reading about *her*, and he'd finally realised that I'd known all along. His face was blank, and the sinister look in his eyes seemed to bore straight through me. I don't think we'd ever had unbroken eye contact for this long, and we were both silent as though there was nothing else left to say. His rhythm became inconsistent; his movements more careless. That's when the pain hit, like a blunt blade stabbing through my skin.

"Shit."

"Fuck, have I hurt you?"

The water began turning red, like those blood oranges I squeezed for him every morning.

"I'm okay."

if there is ever a time

that sore can feel good

this is it

- martyr

"No you're not, you're bleeding."

We got out of the bath and watched the crimson

tinted water swirl down the drain, and I felt the pain ease away simultaneously.

"I'm so sorry," he said, emanating guilt, and tears began to slide down his face. It was unnerving to see him cry, in fact, I think this was the first time his tears had ever fallen in front of me. Perhaps he underestimated my devotion to him. How could he not know that I would unconditionally love him, no matter how many times he drew blood from my veins?

What I really wanted to tell him was:

even pain is a pleasure when it's you
even pain is a pleasure when it's you
even pain is a pleasure when it's you
even pain is a pleasure when it's you

I was as dependant on him as the sun was on the day: I was in too deep. And if he ever found out the lengths I would go to for him, he'd back away - even the sight of my blood had reduced him to tears.

The first time I tasted the toxicity in our relationship was the night he said he preferred me drunk. But he did other things, most of them seemingly too insidious to confront or discuss, that nevertheless left me feeling worthless. I guess tonight was one of those times.

I wrapped my towel round my body, unaware that the bleeding hadn't stopped, and watched as he poured himself a generous glass of bourbon.

We checked out of the motel, dropping the keys in a little wooden box on the reception desk. We threw our bags into the boot of his car and walked to the venue. It was only five minutes away and, honestly, it was one of the only things that helped me retain a sense of normality; the streets, him by my side, the orange glow of street lamps illuminating the way to the bar. If I closed my eyes and focused on the breeze I could almost imagine I was back in Venice. But those thoughts were interrupted by his constant pleads to be absolved. He kept asking if I was okay, if the pain had gone, saying how sorry he was, how he didn't realise he was hurting me.

"Just stop," I said, becoming increasingly exasperated. "It's done with now."

He nodded his head and pouted; our hands slowly fell out of each other's grip. I think this was the first time I had been in control, and there was on oddly unsettling atmosphere. The pain had settled to a dull ache: strong enough to remind me of what had happened, but not too strong to cause me anger.

We walked on.

We're Worried About Him

he is perhaps the most influential man i've ever met

i hate smoking

til i see a cigarette in his mouth

hate the sun

til i see him bathing in it

hate driving

til i become his passenger

he rewrites what i hate

what i love

enchanting me with Venice

and those orange trees

so i think about my parents

and friends back at home

whose faces i haven't seen for months

and ask

what do they think of me now

throwing away everything i am

everything i stand for

just for him

- influence

I watched him on stage, singing songs about me, to people who didn't know us. They were nothing more than drunken silhouettes, dancing in a room furnished with 80s Americana decor and red neon lights. The chequered floors were sticky with spilled alcohol and the room smelled of stale cigarettes and aftershave and sweat. I sat against the bar, drinking an espresso martini, enjoying the music.

"You must be a big fan," commented an elderly man sat next to me; I guess he'd noticed me quietly singing along.

"You could say that," I laughed. How little he knew, how little everyone knew. Here I was, waiting for the man I loved to finish his set so we could move to the next state together, and everyone in this room thought I was merely just another fan.

"My wife loves this guy, so I thought I'd come to see what the fuss was about."

"And where is she?" I raised my right eyebrow: he was sat on his own, and he was tightly gripping the only other drink on the bar. His knuckles sprouted black hair, contrasting the grey running through the heavy fringe that was pushed up by his thick-framed glasses.

"She left me last night."

"Why?" That was the only response I could think of, even though I wasn't sure whether I should have asked, and definitely not sure whether I wanted to know.

"She found me in bed with another man."

The song finished, and people started applauding - one girl even jumped on her boyfriend's shoulder and started screaming an encore. We engaged in small talk for a while, safely discussing topics that didn't involve his wife. After a few more songs had played I began to feel comfortable, and when he mentioned he worked for a publishing company I saw an opportunity and told him I was poet. He told me to send me some of my poetry through so he could have a read and see if he could pull a few strings for me. I grinned wide; it was easy to forget about my own dreams when I was on tour chasing his. Everything I had written in the few months before hand was for him. Then the old guy, whose name I still didn't know, released his drink from his hand. He ran his palm up my thigh, the condensation from the drink dampening my denim.

"What are you doing?" I tried to be stern, but the shock made my voice crack.

"Don't tell me you're not enjoying this," he said. "Why else would you come here on your own?"

I tried to speak, but he grabbed my crotch hard and leaned forward. As I looked at him in bewilderment a shadow fell across his face.

"What the fuck are you doing?"

The next thing I knew the guy was out cold on the floor, with two black eyes and a bleeding nose. I looked up and there he was, knuckles bruised in a palette of purple.

This was the most unhinged I had ever seen him: I had never felt safer.

"Are you okay?" He wrapped his arms around me and squeezed me tight. The entire audience was watching us, and I could feel their confused stares on my skin. The intermittent feedback from the amp was the only thing breaking the silence.

"I'm okay."

He kissed me on the lips. It wasn't one of those heavy kisses that would often lead to sex, or a morning peck he would leave me with in bed. This was more like, *I've got you, forever, and I'm not letting you go, and I'm telling the world right now that I'm yours and you're mine* - one of those kind of kisses. His hands cupped my face, then made their way into my hair. And in that moment that lasted less than a minute, but was interminable in my mind, I felt grounded again. "Come on, we're going."

That night he received a standing ovation.

3. CALIFORNIA NAVEL

We drove along the Pacific Coast Highway, saying our final goodbye to LA and arriving in San Francisco some 460 miles later. It took much longer than taking the Highway 101, but travelling alongside the ocean and white beaches made the hours feel irrelevant.

The coast was no longer in sight - we were deep into the city - and eventually he carelessly swerved into an empty car park. I didn't know exactly where in San Francisco we were; I didn't care. We'd been travelling for over six hours, even at the pace he drove. I was just glad to be no longer moving; to be still. The engine cut and I sighed with relief.

We're Worried About Him

one hand on the steering wheel

the other grips my thigh

air con cold

the friction hot

and everything is just

nonchalant

fine

perfect

almost

even if the earth cracks

swallowing us up

at least we can burn together

at the core

- apocalypse

"I prefer nights like these," I said.

"Oh yeah?"

"Yeah." I was downplaying; I *craved* nights like these. After he'd been on stage all night, sharing his voice with the world, all I wanted was a few hours to feel he was mine again. Because he was the citrus of my life, and I needed both his sweetness and bitterness more than I cared to admit.

"You know, I never thanked you for last night."

"That man? It's fine, he was a creep. I just didn't want him to hurt you."

"No, not for that. For kissing me in front of all those people. I know that must have been a big deal for you." I knew it was a risk, but I had to know where I stood; I had to hear it from him instead of relying on my own feelings and biased intuition. There was a long silence where we both just sat staring through the windscreen; there was nothing around us to see, but my body wouldn't let me look away.

"Look. I don't know what it is that makes you think I'm not comfortable with people knowing about us - maybe you think I'm not in as deep as you are - but I have never *ever* felt any shame in loving you. So stop thinking that." He unbuckled his seatbelt and shifted to face me, and I turned my head so our eyes met. "It's always been you, you know. What have I got to fucking do to prove how much I love you? Because if a beaten up fifty-year old and bleeding knuckles doesn't show it then I don't know what does."

I looked at his bruised knuckles and kissed the purple stain, hoping it would somehow heal. He squeezed my hand tight and pressed his lips hard against mine.

I glowed: that was the first time he'd told me he loved me.

Some nights we fell asleep in the back of his car, too tired to drive around and search for a cheap motel, too tired to care: his guitar case often his pillow, and his chest always mine. It was hardly glamorous, waking up against hot leather, shivering under the tepid water of bar-owners' showers, living off food that could only be consumed by adding hot water. But there was also something innately precious about living on the minimum with someone who meant so much to me.

We spent just over a week in San Fransisco, leaving just before the place became familiar, which I suppose was a good thing. His manager said he'd been asked to perform in Vegas. The venues were getting bigger, growing from small bars that held less than fifty people, to stages with thousands surrounding them. But the fame never seemed to change him; if anything he was unfazed by the popularity, just happy that people were finally listening to his music. He would tell people that he wasn't doing it for the money and they would laugh, as if there was no other reason he would be travelling relentlessly around the country, sleeping in his car and living out of his boot.

It was rare for him to have a night off, but somewhere in-between California and Nevada - by this point I'd lost track of the specifics - the venue had messed up their calendar and weren't expecting him to arrive until the following day. In other words: that night was ours.

"I hate how early it gets dark here," I complained as I opened the petrol cap and shoved the nozzle into his car.

"How much am I putting in?"

"Just fill it up. We have a while to go. Oh, and summer *is* over you know." His reminder stung. It was November now, we were closer to winter than we were summer; yet I was still clinging on to the memories of August. I filled the tank until the diesel cut off, then went to pay while he waited in the car. The haggard woman behind the counter didn't greet me, just snatched the notes out of my hand and shoved them in the till.

"Is that it?" she snarled.

"That's all, have a nice day." I rolled my eyes and

walked out, pushing through the door and letting it bang against the wall. "Rude bitch," I muttered underneath my breath, and I could see him in the car laughing at my thunderous expression.

"So what shall we do?" I fastened my seatbelt, then laid back and let my head sink into the headrest.

"Is it cloudy?" he asked, and I frowned at him in complete confusion. "Great, I have somewhere in mind." He grinned as he answered his own question, a grin that just made my whole body fill with adrenaline. We abandoned the car on an empty street and walked past rows and rows of terraced houses that all seemed to blur together. Since we'd left Venice, everything looked the same: the petrol stations where we'd stop, the venues where he'd sing, the motels where we'd sleep - they were all predictable, lacking in character, and, in every way possible, failed dismally to compare with the beauty Venice held.

We'd been walking for over 15 minutes; there was nothing new in sight and I still had no idea where he was taking me. I was wearing a striped t-shirt he'd worn on stage, and I inhaled the smell of his sweat and aftershave strongly through my nose, wishing for it to remain inside me forever. The wind was up, and when he noticed my goosebumps he gave me his leather jacket, which buried me, but he'd been wearing it when I'd first laid eyes on him, and I cherished it almost as much as I cherished being with him. He sparked up and held his hand out for me to hold. His touch was magnetic, and every time our skin collided I felt the electricity coursing around my body. It was impossible to become accustomed to somebody as magnificent as him.

"We're here!" His sudden excitement confused me: we were in the middle of nowhere. The terraced houses had come to an end about a mile back, and now all that surrounded us were phone-wires strung about the air, and wide roads leading to the freeway.

I looked at him in anticipation but he just kept guiding me forward, until eventually a domed-shaped building came into view.

"An observatory?" I questioned.

"Yes, an observatory," he replied, smirking.

i sympathise with stars

constantly shining

to be ignored in daylight

and only admired at night

loved for the thing

that is killing them

like loving him

and burning out

myself

- fickle

He moved the telescope while I held my right eye to it.

"You see that star there?"

I nodded.

"That's Draco." He shifted the telescope down and slightly to the left and another star came into view. "That's Arcturus, and this…" He moved the telescope up a bit, and gently moved it left until I saw a scattering of stars resembling the shape of a crown: "that's Corona Borealis."

"Wow," I breathed. He let go of the telescope and let me wrap my hands around it, tilting it up until I could see another bright light. "So what's that?"

"That? That's a satellite," he laughed. I started

laughing too, turning to wrap my arms around him, and he hugged me back so hard my feet lifted off the ground. *I had missed this, feeling like we were the only two people on Earth, even though we'd just spent the past hour exploring the universe.*

"I never knew you loved space so much," I smiled; then the realisation that perhaps I didn't know as much about him as I thought I did soon made my face drop.

"You don't like it when I look at you for too long, do you?" he asked. "So I started studying something else. Something that doesn't mind being observed. Something that I know will always be there." His words kind of hurt, partly because they were true, and partly because I never knew he felt like that. I hung my head in shame and stared at the floor.

"Point proven," he observed, lifting my chin up with his forefinger and smiling at me wolfishly.

We're Worried About Him

i'm sorry

for all the times i

look at you

through the reflection of the rear view mirror

unable to turn and face you

sorry for the times i

listen to your words

whilst staring down at my coffee

because i can't bring myself to look up

i'm so sorry

for every time you wrap your arms around me

and i don't keep hold of you

it's just i

never want to get used to your eyes

or your voice

or even your touch

in the fear that one day you'll stop

- reciprocate

Looking at the stars didn't make my problems feel small: quite the opposite. I guess only I could have looked out into the vast universe, realising how insignificant we were, and still have worried about us. The tour was ending in a month, leaving only four weeks of living on the open road, watching him rehearse before those red velvet curtains exposed him to his audience, spending nights like these star gazing and early mornings driving through state borders. There was a part of me that had been praying for this day to come ever since I boarded that plane three months ago - impatiently anticipating our return to Venice so we could relive those summer nights.

But we never spoke about going back to Italy; we never even spoke about the tour ending. We did what we did best, and avoided the fact that pretty soon we'd have to decide what came next. I think the future scared him too, and our shared fear of the unknown made us both complacent in our ignorance.

He was chatting to an elderly couple by two small models of the solar system, and they seemed entranced as they gazed up at him. He towered over both of them so had bent his legs in order to mirror their height. I just stood back and marvelled at his ability to make anyone and everyone fall helplessly in love with him. He really was too pure to be human, a hybrid - so angelic with a hint of darkness that I still yearned to learn more about. His palm was covering Earth, which was somewhat a perfect symbol for how I revolved around him. His phone must have begun to vibrate, because he shoved his hand into his pocket and quickly said farewell to the elderly couple with an effortless raise of one hand.

He was on the phone for at least five minutes, frequently nodding his head but showing no sign of emotion on his face. I became paranoid that he purposefully not looking in my direction, that the news he was receiving and nodding along to was something that could break me if I was to hear it. As I walked towards him, he abruptly ended the call and shook his head regretfully.

"Who was it?" I asked, knowing I wasn't ready for the answer.

"That was my manager. He wants me to stay on tour for another six months." His voice was as ambiguous as his face - betraying nothing.

"And what did you say?" My voice cracked, and my eyes immediately began to burn. We were four weeks away from the end, and now he might have agreed to another six months on the road. America still? Or maybe England? Wherever it was, I didn't want any of it. All I wanted was for it to be over so we could return to Venice.

"I said yes."

I gulped hard, trying not to let emotion overwhelm me. "Of course you did."

I walked away.

He chased after me, but I ignored his pleading voice despite every instinct in my body telling me to turn back to him. Everything had come rushing back: the time I saw him kissing that girl, when he said he preferred me drunk, the sex that made me bleed. Every negative experience I'd ever had with him invaded my mind, and all of those beloved memories we made in Venice were suddenly tarnished forever.

"Let me explain," he yelled, struggling to catch up with me. But I didn't want an explanation; in fact, listening to his justification as to why he would choose the tour over me was the last thing I wanted to hear. The sky was turning black, and thick grey clouds slowly moved above us. If this was my pathetic fallacy then I was dreading the hurricane.

When he finally caught up with me he grabbed my arm and swung me round to face him. I wrenched out of his firm grip and ripped his leather jacket off, throwing it to the ground.

I'd rather have been cold than warmed by something of his.

I wrapped my hand around my left wrist, and I dug my nails into my skin hard enough to feel a piercing sensation - anything to distract me from this pain was a blessing. My chest was tight, and my ribs felt like they were closing in and suffocating me. My eyes closed, sealing the tears that wanted to fall.

"Stop doing that. You're hurting yourself." He snatched at my arm again and pulled me closer to him, making our chests briefly collide together. "You need to calm down."

"No. I think I need to leave." I managed to say the words slowly: it was like I'd been drained of emotion and now I was just tired and cold and wanted to go home - wherever that was. He bit his lip, as though trying to resist saying what was on the tip of his sharp tongue - then he gave in.

"Fuck you. You know, this would never have happened if I'd just carried on fucking that girl. You changed me. You changed everything I knew, and what for? So you could just end it now and live a separate life. It's six months. Six fucking months. That won't matter in ten years. I have to do this, and I need you to understand why I need to do this."

But I didn't want to know. Every bone in my body could have cracked, and still not compared to the agony his words brought. It was excruciating. I dropped to the floor and felt the rough tarmac graze my knees. There was no eye to this storm, no temporary peace amid the chaos: just destruction.

I can't remember how we got back to the car, and I don't recall walking - I assumed he'd thrown me over his shoulders and carried me back. I must have blacked out after I fell to my knees because there were still small bits of tarmac tangled in the hairs of my legs when I awoke.

He was lay along the back seats of the car, head buried in his folded leather jacket. I stayed in the front passenger seat, rigid, upright, looking into nothingness. The ignition was off, so was the radio, but as usual my mind was cruelly wide awake, reliving all those times he made me cry and bleed. The bad thoughts were back; it was a curse to feel things so strongly they had the power to physically torment me.

"You know I never thought things would turn out like this." There was some sincerity in his muffled voice, but he sounded as defeated as I felt.

The next words we spoke were ones I never thought we'd say to each other: I had played this conversation out in my mind time and time again, but never imagined it could turn into reality. And when I realised the enormity of what we were saying, the tears flooded out.

"It's really over, isn't it?"

"I think so."

"I think so, too."

4. VALENCIA

SIX MONTHS LATER

I'd been travelling round Italy during the winter, and as I arrived in Rome I was welcomed by the beginning of spring. I stayed in a district called EUR Rome, characterised by blue skies and white buildings. The architecture there originated from Mussolini's reign, and there was something unsettling about how warm the air felt in a place that looked so cold and clinical. There were no tourists - just like in Treviso, people thought there was nothing worthy here. I walked to the square colosseum, which had recently been taken over by Fendi's headquarters, and spent some time appreciating my new surroundings. A row of prositiues stood at the bottom of the steps. They didn't say anything to me when I walked past, but one of the petite blonde girls who couldn't have been older than 18 looked at my grazed knees and dark eyes and offered a sympathetic smile.

is he worth it?

the bruised knees

bruised neck

bruised mind

- damage

The first few months were difficult: it felt as though I had become so attached to him I was addicted, and I was now experiencing cold withdrawal. I didn't sleep much, and on the off chance I did, nightmares that I couldn't remember afterwards would strike in the middle of the night, staining my white t-shirts with yellow sweat. I avoided contact with family and friends, because I still couldn't quite admit it was over myself, let alone to anyone else. No amount of time could ease the overwhelming physical desire I felt to get him back.

I don't think many people truly move on from the ones they love - they just distract themselves and make changes to feel different. Which is exactly what I did, with flights to places that were slowly getting closer to Venice, empty beaches that allowed me to run into the sea and abandon my belongings on the sand, purple skies and red sunsets that I watched turn to darkness. I was getting better at distracting myself, which I suppose translated to *I'm getting over him*. I swapped my beloved espresso martinis for bourbon on the rocks, dyed my bleached hair black, and stopped wearing his leather jacket, the only physical reminder I had from the night everything went wrong. When I arrived in Verona I walked into an old tattoo studio which accepted walk-ins. Everyone was heavily pierced and tattooed, and my bare skin attracted a few glares that said I didn't belong there. I embraced the pain, savouring every moment of the needle dragging along my skin. All the things I had changed - the drinks, my hair, my choice of clothing - acted as my coping mechanisms, keeping the side effects of losing him at bay, but I knew if I ever felt his touch again I would relapse.

And eventually, the cling film would come off, the tattoo would heal, but the raw pain his missing presence caused would still be there.

Spending so much time on my own was both a blessing and a curse - enabling me to forgive him for all the bad things he did, but allowing me to fixate on how selfish and dependant I had been. I wanted to tell him how sorry I was for the way I reacted, but I hadn't spoken to him since I'd left the States. I watched videos of him online and hoped he'd somehow feel my presence behind the screen.

He was in Texas now, finishing off the last few venues before the tour ended. His fame was greater than ever, to the point that during my brief stay in Naples, one of his fans recognised *me*. Apparently someone had been recording on the night he knocked that guy out, and now it was one of the highest viewed videos of his tour. I agreed

when she told me how great he was - there was no
bitterness left in me anymore. Honestly, I wished him all
the success he deserved, and it was nice to see it was finally
happening for him.

I was staying in an apartment owned by a woman who
used to live in England, but had moved here to EUR
Rome to marry her husband. Knowing she had made such
a life changing sacrifice for love helped me feel more sane
about leaving Venice to be on the open road with him, but
it seemed to have been worth it for her in the end, which
was more than could have been said for me. Her children
were at school during the day, and at night they played out
on the streets, always gathering in large groups near the
Santi Pietro e Paolo a Via Ostiense, a beautifully
intimidating church with a dome so large it was visible to
most of the city. I sometimes drank lager with Maria out
on the patio, despite not even liking the stuff, but she was
one of those people you couldn't possibly say no to. She
never asked why I was there, why she heard me crying
most nights, why my eyes were getting noticeably darker,
and why the cuts on my knees never healed. But one night,
after we had smoked a packet of cigarettes and finished a
crate of lager together, she kissed me on the forehead,
leaving a faint imprint of her dark purple lipstick, and said
"tutto andrà a posto."

Everything will fall into place

Maria threw a small leaving party in my honour when I
told her I was departing for Venice the next day. I insisted
it wasn't necessary, but I still hadn't worked out how to say
no to her. We drank lager with her husband, and the
children tried to drink whatever remained in the glass
bottles at the end of the night. They were closest thing to
a real family I'd had in a long time, and it saddened me to
think I might never seem them again. She ordered pizza
from my favourite pizzeria and laughed one last time at the

fact I didn't have cheese on my pizza. I'd already packed: a note book, his guitar pick, a few clothes and some toiletries were all I carried on my back. Every time I left a different city I threw a few things out - most of my stuff stayed in my suitcase, so I figured I didn't really need it.

That night I put one of his favourite records on, *Asleep* by The Smiths. We would always listen to it in bed, yet now I carefully watched the needle touching the vinyl, hoping it would somehow scratch and the melody would cease. I wanted to re-write our song, because it no longer played like it used to. Those lyrics about not wanting to wake up alone used to resonate strongly with me, but now, even knowing I wouldn't wake up beside him, I was okay.

The next day they waved me off from Roma Termini station, giving me a bag full of leftover pizza and a hand-written note saying how I would always be welcomed back. The coach was empty, apart from an American family that was loudly planning their itinerary. They missed out the best things Venice offered, and stuck to the generic tourist holiday. I sighed, put my headphones in and slept for the next few hours.

And then there I was, not dreaming, not imagining, not reminiscing. I was finally back in Venice, and for the first time in six months, I felt loved.

5. SEVILLE

I revisited all the places I once fell in love with: St Marks Basilica, Piazza San Marco, Doge's Palace, shops that sold Murano glass and pizzerias with steel tables and chairs outside. Nothing had altered; Venice had preserved itself for my return. The pink casa on the river still stood tall, and the same five-foot man with the dark moustache sold magazines in his edicola. While I was on the road I had convinced myself I was romanticising Venice's perfection , but that wasn't the case at all: it was as flawless as I remembered.

Even though I'd been in Italy for a while, acclimatising to the unbearable heat was impossible, and it made my skin turn pink, tender and tight to the touch. The air was always heavy, like a thick fog of warmth that made it difficult to breathe or cool down. Being surrounded by so much water was the city's way of teasing me. The stifling air was tempting me to jump in, to let my clothes cling to my frame and finally feel cool again. Oh, how I'd missed the water. I never felt alone when it was by my side, following my every turn and settling when I came to a halt. I sat down on the edge of an empty street, across from an deserted pottery factory that had closed down a few years back. I took off my shoes and socks and lowered my feet into the water, finding the cold contrast was all I needed.

Tourists had invaded Venice in full force, which meant every restaurant and café was packed full. Even the usually remote spots were busy with English and American accents whining about the heat. It was the only place that was empty: the street turned into a dead end and the stillness of the water caused a stagnant smell to fester in the air, but that seemed a small sacrifice to pay if it meant I could be alone again. My notebook was now filled with poems, enough to publish if I wasn't so scared of rejection: the idea of people reading about the dark parts of my life left me feeling exposed and vulnerable. The last thing I'd scribbled was a poem on the back page of my book, and it made me feel empty when I read it aloud. I wanted him to read it, so maybe he could have seen what my life was like before we had met, and maybe then he would have understood why I reacted the way I did, why I left when things got hard. Why I didn't persevere like I should have.

Like I should have.
Like I should have.
Like I should have.
Like I fucking *should have.*

Liam Gilliver

i spend my teenage years

doing everything i can

to feel

i bleach my hair

til my scalp turns red

drink spirits that make my throat burn

to empty my stomach

sit under the shower

with water so hot

every drop stings

i say yes

when i mean *get off me*

say yes

when i mean *stop - you're hurting me*

so when people tell me that

these are the best years of my life

i hope to god

they don't mean it

just like i don't mean it

when i say

yes

- numb

I peeled the scabs that covered my knees and examined the white skin underneath. Darkness had begun to creep in, and I saw the yellow moonlight hit the canal's surface for what felt like the first time in forever. The glistening water remained overwhelmingly enticing and I couldn't resist its call any longer, so I simply jumped in and held my breath as I plunged underwater. Finally, I felt cold, and my salty tears mixed with the water like I was crying into the city: now a part of me would live there forever, and, if I ever departed, that would be my legacy.

I headed to our apartment with dripping wet clothes and my hair slicked back. It was the one place I'd put off seeing all day. When I left America without him he told me I would always be welcome there, that he didn't think Venice was in his future, and, when the time came that he wanted to buy a house, he'd sell the place. He had inherited it from his uncle, whom he'd never known about until his death, so he had no real attachment to it.

The apartment was waiting for me, just like Venice - untouched and unchanged. Our bed was unmade, the kitchen calendar was still on August, and the letters had piled up in the corridor. I was home. I slept on the sofa that night: something didn't feel right about laying in our bed without him. I didn't know how long I'd be staying there, whether I could live on my own permanently, or whether Venice was even in my future at all. But I was grateful to be back in the place where it had all started, even if he wasn't there.

6. BERGAMOT

It was my first morning in Venice. The sun was shining and the air-conditioning had automatically turned on to keep the place cool. The kitchen tiles were cold on my bare feet, and my clothes were still soaked from the night before.

I busied myself with menial tasks which, for a while, allowed me to escape reality. I hung the wet clothes over the kitchen stools, letting the water pool onto the floor, just so I could distract myself that little bit longer. I retrieved the bunch of letters from the floor and flicked through them, most of them irrelevant junk from months back, which I threw straight into the bin. But the last thing clutched in my hand was an envelope which revealed two postcards when I gingerly opened it, interest piqued. It had a distinctive blue stamp in the top corner that I seem to recognise from somewhere, with the address of the apartment centrally printed in a small unassuming font on the back.

I pulled out the two postcards, one of Central Park and one of the ice rink at Rockerfeller Center, pictured lit up with lanterns and lights, and turned them over; he'd recently done a few shows in New York, and hope blossomed quietly yet surely in the back of my mind at the possible parallel.

"Fuck," I gasped - it was his writing: 'I don't know when you'll read this. I'm not sure where I'll be when you get it. But I hope you're now stood in our kitchen anticipating what I'm about to say. I'm in New York at the moment. You'd love it here. You always said you wanted to work in Manhattan, remember? You wanted to work for Vogue and eat your lunch in Central Park. You said you'd love to go there during the winter, so you could skate at Rockefeller on Christmas Day and watch the ball drop at New Year's.'

I swapped them over clumsily, fingers trembling as my eyes shot down the next card. 'Anyway, I'm writing because I want to tell you that I love you. That there hasn't been a day where I haven't thought about you. Being without you has made me feel crazy, like actually crazy. I'm sorry, I'm so sorry. I'm heading back to Venice when the tour is over, and I hope you'll be there waiting. We can start over, we can be together. I never should have let you go. All my love x'

If only I'd gone straight to Venice: then I'd have known how he was feeling instead of guessing for all that time. Then I wouldn't have convinced myself it was over and tried to distract myself from the pain. And maybe then the scabs would have healed and the darkness under my eyes would have disappeared.

I couldn't help but question whether he still meant what he'd wrote, or if things had changed since he'd sent the postcards and moved on from New York. Was he still the same person I left in San Fransisco? Knowing how much I had changed in the last six months was making me suspect if he had too.

I stuck the postcards on the fridge under a magnet of a gondola he bought me once as a joke. His words had overwhelmed me, to the point where all I could do was pretend I hadn't even read them. I didn't want to get too excited, for it to all fall through in the end: I was only too aware of how easy it would be to relapse. I wiped my eyes and made breakfast as I usually would, waiting for the coffee to heat under the percolator, and the bread to toast: reverting back to my old routine was much easier than getting used to life on the road, a feat I guess I never really achieved. I looked through the window, reuniting myself with the views that had greeted me every morning last summer: the church in the distance, the cobbled pavements on the street below, and locals who still looked familiar as they began their day. But I felt like my eyes were still searching for something that was no longer present, and it suddenly made me feel like something was different.

"Oh shit." My heart sunk as the realisation hit me - the orange trees. They weren't there, the ones I used to pick the fruit from every morning; no longer towering over the apartment and sheltering the patio. They were gone. I ran out of the back door and saw mounds of dirt where the trunks had been ripped from the ground. All that remained were a few dried up oranges, abandoned under the glare of the sun. I dropped to the floor, burying my head in my lap and starting to cry, feeling my knees sink further into the mud with each gut-wrenching sob. It was then I realised everything had changed, and it was solely down to his absence. It was *him* I loved, not Venice.

and

just like the snow

you always return

unexpected

but never unwanted

and when you melt away

know that i'll be waiting

praying the skies turn white

so i can watch you fall from the heavens

in the hope that this time you'll settle

- thaw

I picked up a few pieces of the dried fruit and walked into the kitchen, feeling bits of mud falling off me with each step. I grabbed the phone and dialled his number: I'd wanted to do this since the day I left him, and the euphoria I felt for giving into my addiction was overwhelming.

"Hello?" he answered.

His voice was enough to send me into overdose, and as I replied my knees caved in as if I was about to pass out.

"I love you. I've always loved you. I think if I ever stopped loving you I couldn't live with myself. There's been no one since you. Promise me something: promise me you'll come back. We can buy a house, decorate it, wear denim overalls and throw paint over each other. Not this place, somewhere else, somewhere that belongs to both of us. We can grow orange trees outside, get married in that church with those fucking bells that kept us up all night. I want to grow old with you. I always thought we had to be by each other's side to make this work, you know? But finish your tour, and I'll publish my book, and when we've both done the things we have to do we can come back to each other. And if life throws any more shit at us and we separate again, please know that I've grown and I can deal with it better now. Just promise you'll come back. I can't even try and imagine my life without you; if I had never met you I'd never have known I could fall in this deep. I'd be nothing. I spent all this time struggling to separate my love for you and my love for Venice, and now it's just so clear. It's you. It always has been." I stopped speaking, too overwhelmed with gratuity at finally being able to express my love for him to even think about his response. I inhaled. "I mean, if what you wrote still stands. I —" I stopped abruptly, as the demon on my shoulder reared its ugly head again. What if I was right, what if he had moved on? Had I just poured my heart out for nothing? I braced myself for the sympathy in his voice, steadying myself on the counter.

"Of course," came his voice, and I knew straight away my doubt was unfounded. "I love you - always."
We must have been on the phone for hours, and eventually my tears stopped. I had dried out: there was no reason to cry anymore. This was the beginning of forever; he said everything I needed to hear.

"I love you, Peter," I said.

"And I love you, Ezra."

We're Worried About Him

i could never forget him

he is the salt that etches into my skin

the morning after i run into the sea

the smell of cigarettes that buries into my clothes

no matter how many times they are washed

the dents in my mattress

where his knees sink

he is the light that fights its way through the blinds

every morning

and the darkness that steals across the room

every night

- part 1: impressions

and i realise i will never get over him

not that i even want to

these impressions he leaves

and all that he is

is now part of me

and setting him on fire

would mean getting burnt too

- part 2: acceptance

THE END

ESPRESSO MARTINI

75ml espresso

150ml Vodka

75ml coffee liqueur

1tbsp sugar syrup

ice

shake

strain into a chilled glass

"Wait."

drop a single coffee bean into the centre of the drink

"Perfect."

- your first mistake.

ABOUT THE AUTHOR

Liam Gilliver is a writer and poet from the north of England. His work explores the themes of self-belonging, self-torment, love, heartbreak and sex, and is comprised of fiction and reality.

We're Worried About Him is Liam's debut novel. The storyline was inspired by his visits to Italy, his experiences with men, and the personal barriers he has overcome.

11766343R00037

Printed in Great Britain
by Amazon